Really
Rabbits

Virginia Kroll • Illustrated by Philomena O'Neill

ichi Charlesbridge

To my pets' sensational vets, Drs. Robert Rogers, Sharon Fisk,
Carl Tomascke, Claudia Cataldo, and Susan Mercer. — V.K.

For Paul, who I Really love. — P.O.

Published by Charlesbridge, 85 Main Street, Watertown, MA 02472
(617) 926-0329 • www.charlesbridge.com

Library of Congress Cataloging-in-Publication Data

Kroll, Virginia L.
  Really rabbits / by Virginia Kroll ; illustrated by Philomena O'Neill.
    p. cm.
  Summary: Two pet rabbits sneak out of their cage at night to tidy the
house and do other chores so that their owners will have more time to play
with them.
  ISBN-13: 978-1-57091-897-1; ISBN-10: 1-57091-897-X (reinforced for library use)
  ISBN-13: 978-1-57091-898-8; ISBN-10: 1-57091-898-8 (softcover)
  [1. Rabbits--Fiction. 2. Housekeeping--Fiction.] I. O'Neill, Philomena,
ill. II. Title.
  PZ7.K9227Rea 2006
  [E]--dc22
                                2005020405

Printed in Korea
(hc) 10 9 8 7 6 5 4 3 2 1   (sc) 10 9 8 7 6 5 4 3 2 1

Tulip the bunny waited every day for Grace the girl to come home from school. Then Grace would take Tulip out of the cage, stroke her silky fur, and play with her.

Tulip didn't like being alone every night. She was lonely most of the day too. When Peter the boy brought a fluffy gray bunny home one day, Tulip thumped for joy.

Snuggle was grumpy at first, but he and Tulip soon became great friends.

Together, they told rabbit jokes and played rabbit games.

One night, during a game of Rabbit Round
the Rosy, Tulip got an idea.

"Every day, I see how Grace opens and closes
the door to our cage. I think I might be able
to do it!"

Tulip stretched her paw through the cage and lifted the latch. *Presto!* The door swung open.

"Come on, let's go!" she said.

Tulip raced here, and dashed there, and did flips in the air. Snuggle scurried across the carpet and slid across the floor.

They found treasures everywhere.

"Yum!" said Tulip. "A piece of celery from Grace's dinner!"

"And here's a raisin from Peter's snack!" said Snuggle.

In the morning, an alarm clock rang loudly.

The rabbits hurried back to the cage when
they heard footsteps on the stairs.

Night after night, Tulip and Snuggle escaped and explored.

Soon, they had visited every room
in the house.

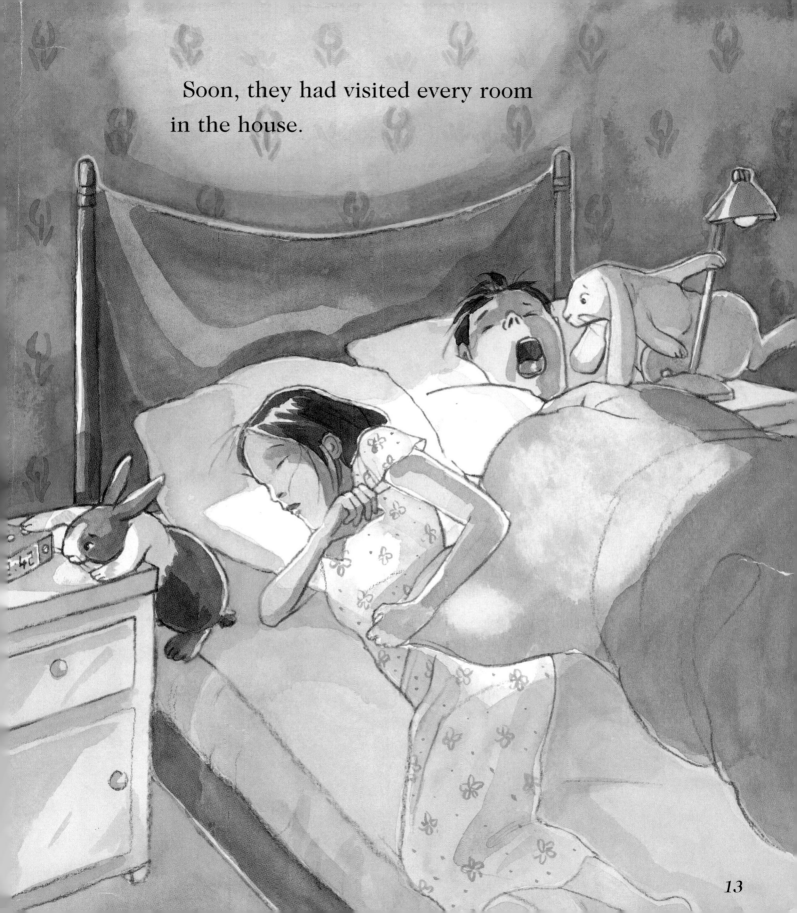

They wanted to try something new.

"I have an idea!" Tulip said one night.

She and Snuggle got busy folding all the
clean bath towels in the laundry basket.

The night after that, they swept the floor.

Another night, they put the toys away . . .

and dusted the
furniture.

The next night, they neatly lined up
the shoes in the back hall.

The children's mother said, "How nice!"

She gave each child a special kiss before they left for school.

One day, Grace raised her eyebrows at Peter.

"Mom sure is happy. I wonder who's been cleaning up."

"Maybe it's elves," guessed Peter.

"Or fairies," said Grace.

"Thank you, whoever you are!"
Grace shouted, hoping the helpers
could hear her.

23

Tulip whispered, "They always think magic is done by tiny people."

"They'd never believe it's really rabbits!" agreed Snuggle.

The next night, Tulip and Snuggle stacked the magazines and newspapers to be recycled.

"You know, our cage could use a cleaning," said Snuggle.

"No way," Tulip said. "It's more fun to clean Grace and Peter's house. Besides, then they'd know it was us!"

So instead, Tulip and Snuggle cooked a tuna casserole.

Grace and Peter's mother was happier than ever.

"Delicious!" said their father. Grace and Peter agreed.

The whole family smiled more and argued less.

Best of all, Grace and Peter had more time
to play with Tulip and Snuggle.

One afternoon, the children's mother said, "Why don't you let your rabbits hop around and explore a bit? They must be tired of sitting all day."

Tulip and Snuggle tried to hide their smiles.

That night they turned on the computer
and looked up ways to make carrot cake.

For Parents, Teachers, and All Those Who Help Children Learn to Read

Part of learning to read is becoming familiar with the kinds of letter combinations we call consonant blends and digraphs. A blend is a combination that includes the sounds of each letter, like the s-w blend in sweet. A digraph is a combination that has an entirely new sound, like the c-h in cheese.

Read the book aloud the first time just for the fun of the story. Point to each word as you read it to help make the connection between its sound and its appearance.

While reading the story a second time, stop before words with a particular blend or digraph so the child can try to read them. Positive responses and encouragement will make it fun.

Page	Blend	Digraph	Page	Blend	Digraph	Page	Blend	Digraph	Page	Blend	Digraph
3	Grace girl from school stroke silky and play	the then with	9	and flips Snuggle scurried across slid floor	dashed there the	15	next morning children's smiled	morning the children's mother thought that	24	whispered agreed Snuggle	whispered they think
4	most brought fluffy gray thumped	being she the when thumped	10	found treasures from Grace's and snack Snuggle	they everywhere	16	next and Snuggle	the washed dishes	25	next Snuggle stacked newspapers cleaning clean Grace	the could then they'd
5	Snuggle grumpy first great friends told and played	together they	11	morning alarm clock rang heard footsteps stairs	the when they	17	swept floor	the that they	26	instead and Snuggle	
6	during round Grace and closes able	the think during	12	and Snuggle escaped explored		18		another they the	28	Grace agreed	mother than father
			13		they the	19	and dusted furniture	the			
7	stretched presto swung	stretched through the latch she	14	wanted try and Snuggle folding clean laundry basket	they something she folding the bath	20	next back	the they shoes	29	smiled and best Grace play Snuggle	the whole with
						21	children's child special left school	the children's mother she each child they	31	children's and explore must Snuggle tried smiles	the children's mother why they sitting their
						22	Grace eyebrows cleaning elves	cleaning			
						23	thank Grace helpers	thank whoever shouted the	32	turned and	that they the